standing all the night through

standing all the night through

poems by

Audrey Poetker-Thiessen

Turnstone Press

Turnstone Press
607-100 Arthur Street
Winnipeg, Manitoba
Canada R3B 1H3

Some of these poems have appeared in *The Mennonite Mirror*, *The New Quarterly*, *Prairie Fire*, *Canadian Literature*, *Scrivener* and *Wascana Review*.

Turnstone Press gratefully acknowledges the assistance of the Canada Council and the Manitoba Arts Council.

Cover illustration: Steve Gouthro

Cover design: Marilyn Morton

Text design: Manuela Dias

This book was printed and bound in Canada by Kromar Printing Limited for Turnstone Press.

Canadian Cataloguing in Publication Data

Poetker-Thiessen, Audrey, 1962-

Standing all the night through

Poems.
ISBN 0-88801-169-5

I. Title.

PS8581.0223S73 1992 C811'.54 C92-098105-4
PR9199.3.P62S73 1992

—for Jack

I would like to thank Victor Doerksen for his advice, and also Dennis Cooley

Who is this that cometh out of the wilderness like pillars of smoke, perfumed with myrrh and frankincense. . . .

—Song of Sol. 3:6

CHRISTIAN: We are going to Mount Zion.

Then Atheist fell into a very great laughter.

CHRISTIAN: What's the meaning of your laughter?

ATHEIST: I laugh to see what ignorant persons you are, to take upon you so tedious a journey, and yet are like to have nothing but your travel for your pains.

—John Bunyan, *Pilgrim's Progress*

Then came the sound of a musical instrument, from behind it seemed, very sweet and very short, as if it were one plucking of a string or one note of a bell, and after it a full clear voice—and it sounded so high and strange that he thought it was very far away, further than a star. The voice said, Come.

—C.S. Lewis, *The Pilgrim's Regress*

Contents

& i want to hear menno

in the dream i watch you

where the thistles grow & dandelions

& i want to hear menno

this is the road
we travelled on
this is the road
waters carved
out of granite
& these are the stones
these are the pebbles
they left behind
they trip our feet
send us sprawling
stuttering on
the essential road
the way our words
catching on each sharp
edged rock our torn
skin our bruises

✧

here is abram paetkau's place
before life moved on

this is abram toews
with wife & son
abram went north
& froze to death
his son stepped
on a bomb & died
in leningrad
his wife came to canada
& fell & broke her hip
& walked with a cane
& died in winnipeg

this is a mennonite church
in nikolaipol
today it is in good condition
it is used for storing grain

here are peter & meta schierling
standing with their children
in flowers   the children escape
they live in uruguay

p froese looked like this
when he came back from exile

by this place where
the first ones came
is an old oak tree
the tree is hundreds of years old
under the tree is a picnic
over the picnic is a branch
with a boy with bare feet
the tree is still there

julius died of typhoid fever
peter died of typhoid fever
anna died young
anna the second went into exile
jakob disappeared
david disappeared
katharina went west
justina went west
they didn't make it west

here we see johann dyck
who has a cow now
a little house
johann dyck has overcome

here mrs driedger & her family
are fleeing   mr driedger
is in the army
he will never see his family again
mrs driedger is fleeing west
in march of 1945

this picture was taken
at pruppendorf near altefelde
in marienburg
five children are on the horse
friesen is holding
the last one on

this was once the home
of hans penner
now it is occupied by poles
a polish girl sits barefoot
on the steps in front
of the house that was once
the home of hans penner

this is a mennonite cemetery
bernhard franz & his daughter
sleep here in christ

here people are sitting
under a red banner
"now life is merrier
now life is better"

mrs gerhard poetker
& her four daughters
i have found a poetker
i have found my name
one poetker girl is
holding an umbrella

& in the silence of the wilderness
my own voice fills my head
with all the things
i have remembered
& all the things
i have been told
& i confess i am a stranger
as all my fathers were
searching for a name
to bring home

—from Gerhard Lohrenz, *Heritage Remembered, a pictorial survey of Mennonites in Prussia & Russia*

✧

to understand one must read
alexander solzhenitsyn

my uncle who once was lost
is telling me his story
with no beginning
& no ending

keh-zhee-be   *keh-zhee-be*
kehzheebe   you understand

    KGB

flat words falling
into the distance
between us failing
the hidden things
searched out
in the spaces in the telling
the ancient things
numbered in pauses

the siege of leningrad
    camps
    mines
    guards
    dogs
ten years in siberia
for the word
by the word of one

only alexander solzhenitsyn understands

my uncle who once was lost
has been to bible study twice
once in russia
once in canada

i have found that which was lost
i have found   i have found

each evening he wells
huge against the sky
the words of the nations
hang in necklaces of fire
around the mountain
of his face
each night i wait
the women of my people
soothing me with
chicken soup   words
whose quiet they
pass among themselves
watching my sleep
see they say *how she*
turns in her quilt
it is a fever
they say & softly
creep from the room
from the power
from the glory
she is only dreaming
they whisper to the waiters
she is calling out
menno's name

✧

not with prayers to the dead
or fasts or vigils
we do not make our way
down passover's stony steps
there is no hair shirt
that adds to our righteousness
or flagellation of the flesh
that saves ourselves from self

the just live by faith

with that word
i kindle a fire
i defy the pope
i vex the devil
i please god

the just live by faith

simon peter crucified upside down
james slain by herod
john exiled to patmos
andrew scourged & hung on a tree
philip stoned
bartholemew flayed alive
thomas the doubter burned
through by a lance &
simon the caananite crucified
thaddeaus beaten to death
matthias stoned or crucified
in ethiopia or colchis

not the first or the last
to die before the world
is redeemed
those who live here
walk in light
& cast long shadows
we have no prophets
or princes
no incense or oblation
only a small moment

that moved on

✧

where do you come from
he asked & i said
do you mean
where do i live
& yes he said what
else could i mean
& i said where i live
is not home
to a mennonite
where do you come from
means this side or that
& then it means
from russia or switzerland
after which it means
the netherlands belgium
& prussia & switzerland
again i explained
to him when he asked
before that i said
we lived in darkness

a.

who is this coming from the wilderness
leaning on her love?

meaning in the beginning
it was a thought
thought hard
almost a vision

there is a light up ahead

like a door
or a bridge
or a fit word
or a yoke
that fits

or unites a common
memory out of foxfire

(we know in part
we see in part
an unsafe journey
but a sure arrival)

not a star but a light anyway

we have reached light
    have not reached day
    follow foxfire
    find graveyards

death cannot celebrate thee
the grave cannot praise thee
out of so many martyrs
how do we live

b.

heimat   no plural   native place   home
homeland

by the molotschna river
on the east
up to the tokmak river
in the north
to the river jushanlee
in the south
only the grass
as high as a man
not a tree not a shrub
only the black felt tents
on the steppes of gog
only the grass
& the eagles crashing
the nogaier riding
the wind

c.

this story is mine

    my promised land
    my jordan river
    my palm branches
    my temple
    my altar

my people sacrificed to baal

in the ukraine
we claimed boers
& nazis by turn
for cousins
with each advance
retreat advance
changing to dutchmen
from deutschmen
& back again

this is how it was said to our fathers
thou shalt not kill

unsre heimat ist dort in der höh

d.

menno is samurai
a kamikaze pilot
menno flies into the heart
of the beast
the word is a mighty
two-edged sword
on the divine wind

e.

the music is elusive
it is flat
german the music

is ponderous   it is

clumsy dancing
in graveyards it is
sun tattered wind
worn it is a diamond
the dirge of the bride
sweet bitter the music
of mennonites is
coal in the furnace
inside me   it is

unforgivable

a parable
in the *martyrs' mirror*
dragging mercy
to greater mercy
the pursued
helping the pursuer
who falls pursuing
through the thin
iced river   it is

dangerous

it waits with an axe
as it calls me home

The Martyrs' Mirror by Thieleman J. v. Braght, a list of early anabaptist martyrs

f.

we pass over jordan
this day to the land
in fire by night
& cloud by day
our men of war
consumed by dust
through the great
& terrible wilderness
we pass by the high way
by the narrowest way
to the land where
stones are iron
& hills are brass
to the land of wheat
& milk & honey
with joshua son of none
we pass over jordan
this day to the land
we pass over jordan
this day to the land

g.

& in that better place
the grapes grew the size
of apples   & the sky
was soft as a woman
after childbirth
& the land rejoiced
& claimed it could have flown
because menno came

but it composed itself instead
the new mount zion
in whose mothering shadow
the father's new jerusalem
would rise four-square golden
where menno could dwell
all his hallowed years
among the golden weaving mime
wheat flowing on the steppe
& in that land

no instrument of music is heard
there is only the voice
        voice
        rising
        falling
heart giving tongue to voice
        finding
voice singing by itself
on the dry steppe

h.

boots crashed down
on the fine wooden chairs
in the parlour
in 1920   he said

he remembers his grandmother
very fat very proud
the parlour entered
only on sundays

they came boots crashed down
on the fine wooden chairs
in the parlour
he remembers

sometimes with the others
who remember ukraine then
the long quiet hours
of the night

to his children he remembers
nothing they remember
what they hear secretly
at the stairwell

they remember hearing
the sin of sodom was
fullness of bread
when the earth was

swallowed up in night
boots crashed down
on the fine wooden chairs
in the parlour   he said

they remember

i.

rise up rise up
my people & flee
like a dove from the east
the world has shattered
the prince of darkness
soughs through your
avenues of birches
& grandmother cries
from a very great distance
she is calling you
from happiness from joy
the stalk of my people
is broken at the head
the darkness has spoken
in rain & wind
in the chaos of the north
& the air is split
with war & famine
only the dead
progress in this story
& i keen on & on
from mount zion *my children*
my children

j.

who is this that comes charging like lunatic israelites
across the deserts of the north

parting the rhine
the dnieper the vistula
crying *blessed*
are the paps that
never gave suck
goodbye to the fields
i used to roam

there is a voice crying
in the places wildness waits
maria is weeping for her children
because they were not

(meaning this is a found poem
written in the before times
by the ones who saw & said
behold i make all things new)

k.

menno is a tribe without samaritans
that devours its people
a wilderness without poets
prophets without profit

the diseased you have not strengthened
you have not bound up the broken
neither have you brought again
those which were driven away
or searched out the lost

a people without a name
a place to locate themselves by
are no people at all
says the poet
there is no naming
my people
there is no christening
my people

wodurch haben unsere eltern sich an gott versündigt

1.

how the faithful people
have become a harlot
a wild she-ass
snuffing up the wind

m.

all right then menno
let us speak vulgarly
in the language of men
you have pissed your golden arc
of fine words
into the gaping mouths
of all your women

pacifist

menno *bruder* you have held
us up daily at the point
of your prick before him
whom prostitutes foretold
who births himself of woman
& is pulled bloody every day
from bloody thighs messiah
of women   emancipator
son of woman

come now & quit this fucking around
car-dealer christianity
says the daughter of menno
let us speak comfortably together
your sins are many
your righteousness is the righteousness
of the rapist   come
menno   repent

many preachers have destroyed
my wheatfield
they have trampled it underfoot
the golden sheaves are flat
the stalks are broken
& the glory of menno has fled
before the stink
of his hypocrisy

komm sünder we will talk plain
with the wine & the *tweeback*
under the sugar tree
i confess i am lonely for you
a woman lonely
for her first lover
i want your kiss son of man
though your sins are scarlet
but the harvest is past
the summer has ended
& we are not filled

n.

i am the preacher
the daughter of menno
the storyteller to grandfathers
the teacher of old women

let the elders come forth
from their houses
let them call to me
in the yellow air

that the calf is fattened
the *vaspa* is set
& i am no longer
a stranger among my people

o.

in the summer laughter
ghosted long after
the children were in bed
sometimes you hear
a night bird
sometimes the crickets

    i tell everyone
      it was so
        it was so

i do not exaggerate

in the summer we had a golden life
    i say

you can get lost
in the winter
& die a dozen steps
from home

everyone has a story
he cannot tell

we are lost
we don't know
why we're here
we don't know
if it matters
but it might
it might

summer sunday evening poem
a window open
to the night
a car backfiring
a party a way away
carrying the night across
bernie playing the guitar
thank you thank you ron
the light in the moths

father

lost look

thou

here i am
here i am

father

p. *oracle*

find the lost people
write the found poem
write the lost poem
for finding the lost people

q.

for a long time i have held my peace
i have been still
have restrained myself
now i will rage from my place
i will make my words fire
& my people wood
i will make a legend
out of cabbage soup
& a history out of crockinole
i will spin folk dances
from the catechism
when i gather the scattered
when i remove the *eltesta*
by myself i have sworn
i will lead you
in the dance o my people
i will teach you
when we dance the legend
the geography of our love
& you will buffet the grave
with your laughter
when i annul your covenant
with death when i abolish
the ban when i make
the argument with the grave
of no account

r.

then i will proclaim
that menno is a joyful singer
his song is a ship
on the sea of death

in repetition
menno's words become wings
they become white weddings
white mournings
become our skullcap *our rosary*
our rosary our prayershawl *our ikon*
they become our ikon
against the night

menno sings counterpoint
to death

(o wie schell flieht doch die zeit
o wie schnell flieht doch die zeit)

menno repeats himself
chews his cabbage twice
he does he does

we repeat ourselves
chew our cabbage twice
we do we do

s.

mennonite hymns
were made for dancing
pale on darkness
on terraces of brick
on hot summer nights
they were made for dancing slow
cheek to cheek dancing
for the bearded
& the beardless men
to glide graceful as doves
with their wives
mennonite hymns were made
for women touching men
in the heart on beds
scattered with lilacs
mennonite hymns were made
to be danced to
beside the red river
down in the valley
valley so low
mennonite hymns were made
with the full moon
in the eastern trees
pale on darkness
they were created
apart from the world
on the eighth day

t.

wait for me menno
where the waters run

into the sea my brother
i am coming

to you   carried along
on the strength

of your song i have
    missed
            you

i have missed
you   often

menno brother *bruder*
i have missed
your bright ocean
sky/steppe

your bright eye
deflected off evil

your red neck
damp with sweat

&

hay seeping
from your pores menno
my fair one
on the body

which is broken for me
now i dance
now i lay me down
to milk from your
hairy breast
the knowledge of life
& climb to god
from here

i would

fuck you dry
of your pilgrim song
& pour it out
on troubled waters
to smooth the way
for your children
to come home

i would come home too

u.

i have crossed this wilderness before
i have seen it empty
& have dreamt it filled
when asleep
& when awake

colour me with the red
wrath of the winepress
the blood of women
with black *heimatlieder*
armbands kerchiefs
call me a child birthed
by a wild mare
woodscolt

i begin confession
after the need has passed
i am a stranger wandering
with no burying place
no resting place for my head

colour me menno

night blue in menno's eyes
now & the end of time
is only a moment
of erring astray
in menno's eyes
his protesting eyes

v.

menno is a red flower
blossoming from grandmother's
black hat

menno is haiku
joy cometh by surprise

w.

i will open my mouth
in the low german tongue
surely i will prophesy
unto you my beloved
that menno's beauty is eternal
his house without end
i will woo you with words
my lover my beloved
i will say that mercy reigns
in menno's fields day
into day as the bright
rising of the daystar

x.

komm mol   wua etj
sett es daut woam
vom wachte   weenstens
komm   wel'we toop
räde aus wie deede
aum aunfong

ons wajch es root
met bloot   naut
von trohne   betta
en soltich   ons
noh hüs   es emma
wiet wajch   oba komm

blooß en wel'we toop
gohne noh onse breeda
noh daut bleiwe wota
beffel ranne doahan
noh jesundheit
unja den läwesboom

wel'we ons üträde
met ahm wems vesprätj
es met veeh   met
niefundlaund fesch
wua nacht es dach
en aumsel sinje

emma aus klock fiew
zemorjes   komm mol
wel'we toop gohne
noh daut wuat   noh ons
noh hüs   wua dee
jemeende aula lache

dee tjleen-jemeenda
dee chortitza   breeda-jemeend
woare daunze   en een
tjleenet mejaltje
woat ahn leide

y.

the voice said cry & i said
what shall i cry? all flesh is grass
but the word is forever

there is time before dark to visit
the burying ground to plant marigolds
to watch the heat lightning
it is time to study the shapes of
the stones their leaning their bent
their hard hard kisses

only let me steady myself
on the rock for a minute
give me a minute
just a minute
to catch my breath
& then i will come again
i will start back
i will come home

on the wings of the morning
thighs crippled
by his touch
totally without
wholly empty
a womb without

z.

a long cool man in a white robe

awake in the dark
the morning star bright
in the east

father

lover

my son

my son

this day have i begotten thee

the sound of my lover's steps
toward home
my lover coming home

✧

they still are as
i remember them
comforting   right
it is not easy
resuming this affair
with menno

(here is the church
there is no steeple
i go to the church
to look at the people)

thief in the night
i hide in the faithful
among the old grandmothers
i disguise myself
in the black dress the saints
wrapped themselves in

(is my lord a woman
that he should care
about his children)

i have eaten *vaspa* with menno
in the presence of his wife
i have anointed his feet
poured oil from
an over-flowing cup
in the presence of deacons

he is my lover
i will meet him anywhere
strength is with menno

joy is with fire
every aching wanting
to fill every hole

in careful photos
large-rumped women stand
inside long black dresses
men who might be young
or old   sit straight
in straight-backed chairs
they do not smile
through their faces
or their backs
the way to the altar
still burns with blood
& tears & the wanderers
wander yet   with earnestness
of god   & no fixed
destination

✧

& i want to hear menno
cry out loud

from beneath me
& watch his startled peace

when i enclose him
all day long i want

him to be only
with thoughts of me

for once i want
to be on top

& i want to see menno
face to face

in his face i want
to see him see

what he has missed
not loving me

menno   *come*
tenderly i will ride you

your lips cracked open
sunflower seed

by my tongue & all
your noisy mummery quelled

with raging love
only have faith

& i will sing to you
the front singer

of the *gemeinde*
a song of songs

menno your prick is
the strongest branch

on a strong tree
you hide in me

(i am the tree
green with wind)

& when i thought he loved me
i felt all my skin
was pulse & nerve
my skin ached for the promise
i was a woman without shame
i hinted of other lovers
better offers i greeted
him naked behold i stood
at his door & knocked
my reproach bored him
& i mistaking it for
a lover's teasing
cajoled him with one
coy trick & then another
o i was bitter for myself
my weak woman's eyes
overflowed but he did
not betray his arrogance
look i told him had i
birthed you had you sprung
wet from my thighs
virginal or not
you would have suckled me
like a lover my son my son
song of my flesh
menno had i birthed you
i would have taught you
to love

remember our generations
remember when we burned
& where we buried
remember the windmills caught
the sun each morning held
back the flood once more
remember the sky blue burning
over the steppes white
unto winter remember
the woman's soft cry the child's
coming pink & new
the man black with harvest
his pale forehead hatless
in the evening the kerosene
lamp lighting home remember
the new carrots the new beets
the sunflowers the summer
pale with heat remember waking
remember the bride walking
before the congregation
her love an ache in the blood
remember that remember
the guile the sex in the feather
bed warm the snow outside blowing
cold remember the old woman's
hands the spots the tender skin
the needing wanting remember
the one face only that you
long for the grains of corn
dropped in the earth the children
remember the child's crying
by the green tree the kiss
that makes all things well
the clanging cowbells the low
german tongue the love that forgives
remember

in the dream i watch you

i have dug everywhere
for my dead
i have dug with metal
detectors for the gold
in their teeth
for their yellow hair
with garden trowels
with shovels
i have turned earth
in spades for a sign
of their leaving
i have not found
a note yet
where they passed

but i will not ask him *why*
when a wind leafs
through the boneyard
& the ants carry away
the spots of old flesh
& the beetles polish
the bones for the new
& the spiders stitch it
all together
when my friends live
where i can touch them
now & then to make sure
they're there
i will forgive god
anything then
when it's so
if it's true

my grandmother will tell you
a story if you ask
she will tell you
she will settle back
into her chair
her feet will fold themselves
on the rag rug
& the light will become lamp
the sixty watts
a flame of peas
her hands shelling shadows
smooth green shells
between her thumbs
running down their insides
loosening all their seeds
to winter the fir trees
tossing their shadows
through the window
their dark shapes
bending her voice
she will begin in low german
a word or two in english
my grandmother will tell you
when she settles back
into her rocking
she will begin
our common life
our creation
my grandmother will tell you
when you ask
the old old story

a seer a prophet
like of old times
a poet wandering
in his desert mind
sometimes it is
a small still voice
sometimes the whirlwind

always it is on the brink
of seeing true
a reason for every life
& every death
& brink of death
everything lies under meaning

deep laughter rocks its way
from him sometimes
screams to god
the niverville cedars
are blowing blowing
tearing in the terrible wind

he is following mulroney
following my uncle
following voices
waves beating back
to the sea
childhood from the knotted side
in hymns sung backward

my uncle i would lower you
through the rooftop
of heaven i would
believe for you a light
a little light
in the harbours
of your mind a silence
where no cedars blow
where no angels speak

she tries to tell him
this is one thing
hold on to it   like when
she was a girl she never
missed a dance   she picked
black-eyed susans   & tiger
lilies were wild as then

dancing & life   when did it
all become wrong
when she gave in to him
& put on her shoes when she hung
out the wash   or when
he became a deacon   making her
a wife with a dryer
& a deacon

who needs a dryer when
her strong thin line binds
trees together   keeps the leaves
from unravelling   the sound
wind makes against her apron
gathered for clothespins
the sound of her hair rushing
free from its bun
this fine wind   clear heat
& sunshine trapped forever
in the sheets between two
chokecherry trees

ice cream
pails fill
ed with wild
plums dark
ling after
day long
picking
stumbling in
almost sleep
we leave
homing in on
car & mother
driving the
night through
lights of
past worlds
in complete
silence

✧

the saints
    in grandma's dream
        call *heea heea*
            this is not what she expected
                from tongues of angels

the great spinning wheel
    she is climbing
        is not jacob's ladder
            there is nothing sacred
                about these cows
                    those black & whites
                        moving across the landscape

in this dream she keeps
    a collection
        old empty clouds
            birds' nests
                used hymn books
                    seashells from the coast

down by the river
    chariots of fire roll
        down the red
            it is elijah all over again
                the horses running
                    grandma trying for heaven
                        the saints keep calling
                            the wheel keeps turning

✧

in the dream i watch you
come to me
you are coming
i am staying

in the dream you say *hello*

& your smile is the smile
of the living
i nod to the angel beside you
i will not be fooled again
into hoping for resurrection

you are dead   *sorry*
you are dead   *please*

wordless i turn away & turning
catch your eye again

susie   i ask

you nod & i am coming gently
i touch your flesh
i tell your bones
i measure warmth
you know i have always loved you
i say or you say
i cannot be sure
& knowing you cannot stay

in the dream i watch you
come to me

there is no knowing
you by that river
angels walk
in that great gathering
there is no finding
you   the songs
saints sing hiding
my loud calling
i will meet you
by the gate of judah
in the north
of the city of god
(by the river we will
discover our others
later   the tribe
of our own)
i will know you—
the wind of our finding
will saw through
the trees of life
i will silence the saints
by the river
in my own flesh
i will shut them up
when i find you
when my bones utter
your name

& then i held you again
in the land of the living
from the valley of bones
i watched you return
& we fished out the sun
as we lay by the river
as we lay with the earth
that taught us to dance
we danced
with your children
with their legs
full of laughter
& we sang
as we'd sung
in the aeons before
to the father
in the father's house
we'll go no doubt
tomorrow

grandma & grandpa
dancing on the night
harder the fiddler
calling the dance closer
the moon open
through the barn doors
the moonshine calling
their steps becoming
one step two-step three
grandma dipping
her black skirts
the night calling
grandpa closer
wrapping his legs
in her black skirts
closer & closer

& in that warm place
where our feet scratched
hieroglyphs of childhood
judy still wraps
her only legs
around the swing pole
we laugh & laugh
like the killdeer
with the broken
unbroken wing
& follow the leader
among the stiff september
stalks that glow
with seeds of summer
& it is riding
the long thunder
being a stranger
again

✧

in the legends of my people
the rivers run red
with blood i wept
& dreaming i dreamt
i anointed new flowers
with clay from the grave
& with spittle
& her face was as strange
as the flowers
& i said by the by
i am searching
& she told me again
of the saviour
as she did in
the summers before
& i wept in the dark
as she held me
& dreaming i dreamt
i was found

✧

like earth
women sound grudgingly
keep their secrets
secret disguise
their language
wear consonants
from father tongues

    my first word
    was the sound
    of water mother
    washing the floor
    in low german

men's language
i learned on my own
the hard way
chronicle by chronicle
in church
& by the hair
on men's testicles

but now & again
words slip out
blue & wet
drop their syllables
forked in mothertongue

setting the times
& the seasons
for the planting
& the ingathering
bursting forth
a mighty river for healing
bleeding life
into the earth
a surprise unlooked for
& followed for days

where the thistles grow & dandelions

& i woke to the sound
of my jewish lover singing
high german hymns outside
my bedroom door
all night every night
he carolled of heaven
he gave me no peace
day & night he followed
with old promises
talk of mansions
jesus my friends warned
me about you
he is not like other lovers
they said he will
never leave you
his touch will consume you
he will be a fire in your belly
he will ache in your bones
when he does not come
as he promised
when he tarries
they said as he called
even then through the door
audrey audrey i am waiting
& i shook like a virgin again
as he entered
as the lightning flashed
from the east to the west
i woke to the sound
my jewish lover singing

✧

out of the earth
we made our first legend
& the first woman
(a one-man woman)
staunched blood
from failed seed
with moss from the trees
& the skin of dead animals
sometimes she blessed I Am
sometimes she cursed
& sometimes her muscles ached
from the hoe
from the man
& the first woman
invented prayer
(in the shape
of a wish)

& she named the prairie grasses

 & the coyote
 & the rattlesnake
 & the blood
 & the son
 & the wind
 & the whippoorwill

the man tilled
& broke the earth
into patterns of harvest
& rest from the harvest
& he marked his place
with urine & feces
that the animals might
know who was man
& he ploughed that his furrows
were straight & would
not shame him
if a son of his flesh
would follow the furrow
if his seed would take
root with the rain

& he named the fire

        & the fox
        & the gopher
        & the crow
        & the wheat
        & the field
        & the rain

because words are holy
& terrible weapons
what was left
they named together
(the flicker of fireflies
the moon rising)

when twilight fell
they watched I Am
he shifted in the shapes of

the prairie grasses
the coyote
the rattlesnake
the blood
the son
the wind
the whippoorwill

the fire
the fox
the gopher
the crow
the wheat
the field
the rain

in the garden
he played mysteries
upon his pipes
stags scraped the velvet
from their antlers
off on him

then they named god
the first woman
& the man together

they took the aspect
they could almost see
& named him

& then there were no more prairie
grasses left to hide the coyote
the rattlesnake & the woman's
straining blood as she crouched
to give birth to the son
in the grasses where the wind
& the whippoorwill used to sing

& there was no fire to warm the man
& to keep the fox the gopher
the crow (which are no more)
from the wheat (which grows no more)
the man planted in the field
(no more) to wait for the rain
(which is no more)

they made a poem
out of everything
they had named
out of existence
there is nothing left to name
is how they started the poem off
we have named god
the first woman wrote
in a flare of fear
in the poem
(the first poem)

these are the things that protected us

god

prayer

knowing you would die

fire

wild animals

knowing each time you made love
or fucked (i forgot—they also
named these things separately)
you could have conceived a child

something protected us when we were young

we knew magic is culled
from the body of god

earth sky

fire water

once upon a time
mammoths & sabre-toothed tigers
stampeded through the spaces
of god's teeth
we named them
& now they are gone
& he is dead
god is dead

the first woman said as they sat
where the tall tall grasses
used to grow

from now on
we find our way
by aberrations

from now on
we glimpse
him   only

in stillness

searching for that
former brightness

all
our
days

calling his name
into the void
only the smallest
speech

echoes
back

maria is dancing
dancing on the rock
her white hands touching
stroking the dark
her breasts bouncing
heavy heavy
with her milk
sagging on her heart
ewe upon the hill
white upon the rock
maria dancing
her legs folding
into prayer opening
eye has not seen
ear has not heard
tender she burns
she hears she burns
there she burns
on the rock

woman made from the earth
made life
from the rib of the man
by the breath of god
in the field
the woman sweating
the land
thinning the beets
the woman on polder land
finger in the dam
stopped the flood
on the steppes
in the shadow of death
planted the trees
in the beginning
without form
out of the confusion
the clods
the woman turning the earth
& the stones
shaping the land
to the image of man
the woman made flesh
from the field
is a beet
is a tree
raising the son of man
from the earth
& sweat on the field
god made woman
with the rib
of the morning
live god said
live

owe no man anything

they toil not
neither do they spin
is not life
more than meat
& the body
more than raiment

let not man put asunder

call no man your father

(i speak as a man)

woman
why weepest
thou

in me he came slowly
for a long time
i moved slowly
slowly we moved
each other
measuring debits
& credits
balances due
like thieves
like dancers
circling each other
in a borrowed garden
vipers rise up
on legs & lift
their voice in song
we come like gods
we come we return
before falling
we come falling
into each other
i am not easy
i have heard rumours
death has invented
dreamless sleep
is there place
for a woman
in your life
i ask him
it is only my name
that he speaks
in the garden
the only answer
the only word

his eyes hot
& pitiless
wolf standing over
the kill now
he is prowling
heaven & hell
he is higher
than a kite now
he is flying
he has shaken off
the splinters of
the cross now
he has thrown away
his shroud now
he is naked
& full of rage
he is not bearing
wrongs now
he is so delicate
so fine
so extreme
he is not meek now
with a bent neck
& eyelids humbled
he is burning
his pierced hands
strong as hammers
sharp as chisels
he has chiselled
the cross into
a victory sign
he is so free now
he is not dead now
he is risen

✧

being lost before
i know found

because of you
i am weak
because of you
i am strong

the strength
& the weakness
are round

                    round

penis
cunt
mouth
in a vowel
in an oh
                    oh
                    oh

                    love

i curve about you
i cleave
body to spirit
love to vowel
until morning beats
between my thighs
& grace

                    stillness

when you hide in me

by the river
he washes me of all
the other lovers
until before him
there is no one
with his mouth
tasting of wine
his mouth on mine
together   jesus
how strong his arms are
strong enough to hold
my world sweet jesus
flesh of my flesh
bone of my bone
i take him in
take him in & in & in
until all else is
vanity is foolishness
i like him looking
at me i like what
i see now i am so
blind

& it is strange
how we turn to
each other in sleep
& it is strange
how our bodies
know each other
    we turn out
    that we might
    turn in
    we back away
    that we might
    draw near
though we are blind
we guard against the night
a four-armed beast
love seeks love
tender-eyed in sleep

& i am a child, a child dancing
on this journey
in the beginning
all things begin
pawned to the grave
i close the gap with words
build altars of sound
strike every rock speechless
like moses i must begin
at the beginning
i must write
the story of my death
separated from you
i search the high mountains
& every hilltop
& all burning bushes
i question
following peculiar pillars
i stumble over every serpent
but i am a child, a child calling
an after-the-fall child
a child with naked memories
i look for you
then hide myself
but i am coming, lord
i am coming

✧

where the thistles grow & dandelions
püst at summer's end

in the valley of cranes
i lead my lover to the place

wild roses choose each year
to flatter bees from kleefeld

i lead my lover to a green valley
by gardens of flowers

by stony brooks
i offer my lover a windmill

a house built of sod
i give him

whose eyes are the waters
all waters enter

whose feet are bronze
each toe a light

a sign in the sun
my lover's thighs are two straight roads

that lead only home
my lover's navel is a gravel pit

in moonlight   all lovers
bring their lovers there

my lover is one raindrop
on one pine tree

on one summer day
at silberfeld i lay my lover

down in the graveyard
his white hairs sing & thrum

like a telephone pole in january
& my lover washes

my bones clean with his tongue
with his shaking

with the thunder of his coming
with his word

the dead rise

✧

standing all the night through
we heap these stones
four & five
deep the world
within the circumference
these stones slash our hands
with clear heat

there is blood on the horns
of the altar
blood on the bottom
the altar dripping
down the scarred rock
& filling its dark
pocked surface

there is no redemption
without blood

there is no forgiveness
only the pale light of dawn
catching the knife
on the morning sacrifice
the silence of the souls
under the altar of god
& we are clean again

Translations

unsre heimat ist dort in der höh—our home is on high—from a hymn

wodurch haben unsere eltern sich an gott versündigt—from the catechism—how did our fathers sin against god

bruder—brother

komm sünder—come sinner

tweeback—Mennonite double buns

vaspa—Mennonite lunch

eltesta—elder

o wie schnell flieht doch die zeit—how quickly time passes

heimatlieder—homeland songs

gemeinde—congregation

heea—dear

püst—blow

translation of the low german poem, part x of "who is this coming from the wilderness," page 42

come now   the place
where i sit is warm
with waiting   please
come   let us reason
together   as we did
at our beginning

our road is red
with blood   wet
with tears   bitter
& salty   our
at home   is always
far away   but please

come & let us go together
to our brethren
to that bluest water
buffalo run to
for their healing
under the life tree

let us speak ourselves dry
with him whose treaty
is with cattle   with
newfoundland fish
where night is day
& meadowlarks sing

always as they do
at five in the morning
come now   let us go
together to that word
to our at home   where
the congregations laugh

the small congregation
the chortizers   the mennonite
brethren will dance
& the littlest girl
will lead them

The Cover Artist

Steve Gouthro was born in Picton, Ontario, in 1951. He received his BFA from the University of Manitoba and his MFA from the University of Washington. His work has been shown in numerous solo and group exhibitions in Toronto, Winnipeg, Calgary and Seattle, and is included in collections of the Government of Manitoba, Manitoba Arts Council, Canada Council, Canada Post Corporation and the Winnipeg Art Gallery. His painting *Near the Forks* was chosen for the Manitoba stamp for the 1992 Canada Post Corporation's 125th birthday of Canada issue. Currently, Steve Gouthro teaches at the School of Art, University of Manitoba.

Recent Poetry from Turnstone Press

Agnes in the sky by Di Brandt

this only home by Dennis Cooley

You Don't Get to Be a Saint by Patrick Friesen

why isn't everybody dancing by Maara Haas

saving face by Roy Miki

Hoping for Angels by Patrick O'Connell

Something to Madden the Moon by Brenda Riches

Without Benefit of Words by Kathleen Wall